OLYMPIC DREAMS

by Dan and Janet Ahearn

illustrated by Larry Johnson

TABLE OF CONTENTS

CHAPTER 1

OPPOSITES

Almost everyone agreed that Debbie Flannagan was the best all-around athlete in school. Even boys admitted she was talented.

"Deb's pretty good," they said. Then they'd add, "For a girl." But none of them dared to race her.

Deb did well in all sports, but she was best at running. She flew like a rocket down the soccer field, her bright-red hair streaming out behind her. In softball, she had speed on the base paths. She could stretch a single into a double without a problem.

No one was surprised when Deb was named captain of the girls' track team. She was the champ in every race she ran. She preferred the shorter races. She'd say, "Anything longer than 800 meters and I get so bored. After that, I forget that I'm supposed to be running. You know?" Of course, she didn't mean it. She could do anything.

There was a group of kids who hung on her every word. It was like she had her own cheering section. So nobody would argue that Debbie Flannagan was the best athlete in school.

Nobody, that is, but me.

Mara Hamilton was not at all like Deb. When Mara moved to our seaside town, she and I hit it off right away. Mara liked going with me to the beach to look for creatures the tide brought in. I guess I am what some kids would call a science geek. Mara was not a geek. She was just a good student. Nobody but me knew that she was a great runner.

Every day Mara and I would run along the beach. I'd be huffing and puffing. Mara would be way ahead of me. She'd want to run again and again. She wanted to go as fast and as far as she could.

One day at the end of the summer, after we'd caught the biggest crab ever, she told me in a whisper, "I want to go to the Olympics someday, Benny. I want to win the gold medal."

CHAPTER 2

DIFFERENT STYLES

The next fall, Mara decided to try out for the school track team. Naturally, she made it.

Mara kept up with Deb as they ran around the track. In every race, Mara and Deb ran side by side. Deb still won in the end, but Mara almost beat her. The funny thing was that Deb didn't consider Mara competition. I could see, though, that Mara was gaining on her. But Deb acted like she didn't care.

She'd pat Mara on the back and say, "Think you'll ever catch up to me, Mara?" And Mara would say, "Maybe someday, Deb. Maybe with a lot of practice." Then Deb would smile. "Well, that's the difference between you and me. I don't need a lot of practice." Then she'd walk away, her red ponytail swinging behind her.

Anyway, for a long time, I liked being the only one to notice Mara. It was like I'd discovered a new kind of beetle or

something, like I knew something that no one else knew. You know that kind of feeling? Where you're sure that someday soon everyone else will know and you can say, "I knew all along!" It sounds kind of selfish but it's the way I felt.

Soon, though, I started to resent the fact that no one seemed to notice how great Mara was. Everybody always cheered for Deb, practically before she even laced up her shoes. While Mara ran lap after lap around the track, Deb would be clowning around in front of her fans in the grandstand.

And it's not like there were just a few fans. There were tons of them. They all hung around after school to watch her. And there would be Deb, posing with her new sneakers or warm-up outfit. To top it all off, some of the football players had started to hang around, too. They were making jokes and acting like it was a party. For some reason, that really made me angry.

I was always there, of course, holding the

stopwatch and timing Mara and writing her times down in a notebook. She'd tell me over and over again how grateful she was. I was glad to do it for a friend. It was fun.

Mara and I came up with a scientific training schedule. I think I studied every nutrition book on the planet. I concluded that the best diet included grains, vegetables, fruit, meat or fish, and dairy every day.

Mara had to cut out sweets. So I did, too. With Mara, even giving up my favorite foods was fun. And Mara was getting faster and faster.

One afternoon during a workout, Mara ran

the 400 meter in her fastest time ever (as they say, her personal best). I was shouting and laughing and going crazy. I was as happy as if I had done it myself. I looked around the track to see who was watching. I wanted to brag and shout out the exact time so that everyone could hear. But no one was watching Mara; they were all crowded around Debbie Flannagan. Mara walked up and held out her hand for the notebook.

"How fast?" she said, between deep gulps of air.

I barely heard her. I was too busy staring at Deb and her groupies. "Look at that," I said.

Deb had one heel up on the rail of the chain-link fence and was pretending to stretch. Personally, I think she was just trying to show off her new electric-blue running suit.

"Look at what?" Mara said, taking notebook out of my hand and running her finger down the page to compare her times.

"Deb Flannagan," I said in disgust.

Mara looked up and watched the repulsive spectacle for a moment.

"Yeah," she said, "cool running suit."

And she turned to study the notebook again. I started laughing. Mara was really something.

After checking out her times, Mara started in on the next phase of her training program— her mile run. As Deb and her fans left for the day, I heard Deb call out to Mara.

"Hey, Mara! It doesn't matter how hard you try, you'll never catch me. I'm a One. You're a Two."

Mara was such a great person. She seemed cool about it. She smiled and kept running. I wanted to throw up. Just then the track coach, Ms. Daltry, came jogging by.

"Hey, Benny! How's she doing?" I showed her Mara's times. "Her numbers are really looking good."

Ms. Daltry caught up to Mara. She talked to Mara as they ran. Ms. Daltry is the expert on the pep talk. She could talk a chicken into doing algebra. I sat in the grandstand and read social studies. Does anybody really care how many cranberries are grown in Massachusetts?

Later, Mara told me that Ms. Daltry had told her that all her hard work would pay off once the season began.

"She said I was setting a great example," Mara said. "Who could I be an example for?" I didn't say a word. (But her name is...DEB FLANNAGAN!!)

Deb called Mara "Two" all the time at practice. Everyone acted like it was an honor to be Deb's runner-up. Mara didn't mind. But I did. I didn't think Mara should be in anyone's shadow.

Anyway, Mara still kept up her training all through the season. She became stronger and stronger. By the third track meet, Mara should have been able to beat Deb. But she didn't. Sure, she ran good races. She stayed with Deb the whole way, far ahead of the other girls. But every single time in the final stretch, Mara faded and Deb pulled away to win.

Then Mara would congratulate her and Deb would smile and say, "Let's go celebrate." Mara seemed happy to be second best. It was killing me, I can tell you. I worked hard at this, too, you know.

I was fed up. I finally said something to Mara. "Look, Mara, I can't figure out why you never win a race."

She just smiled and shrugged.

"I don't get it! Deb hardly trains at all. You should be beating her!"

"Oh, Benny," she said, "I don't know. I just don't want to do that to Deb."

"But I thought you wanted to win a gold medal someday. You'll have to run to win."

"This isn't the Olympics," Mara told me. "These are just school races."

"I can't believe you won't try to do your best!"

"I'm doing this for Deb," Mara said.

"Why?"

"She told me her parents expect her to win or they make her life miserable."

"That's not fair to you," I argued.

"You know I could win if I tried."

"I *don't* know!" I said. "You never try! Maybe you *can't* beat her. Maybe it's just easier never to try."

Mara glared at me. Then she walked away without a word. I wondered if I had ruined our friendship. I felt terrible.

CHAPTER 3

STEADY DOES IT

The All-City High School Track and Field Meet is a very big deal. It's in the middle of the season. Schools are invited based on their teams' rankings in our city. That year, for the second time ever, our school made it. Everyone in town was really excited about it.

The day of the trials for the All-City, kids from our school crowded the stands. When they saw Deb, they cheered, "Go, Go, Number One! You're the best under the sun!"

Then, when they saw Mara, they cheered, "Go, go, Two! We're rooting for you!"

I hadn't seen Mara since the day I'd given her a hard time about not trying her best. She seemed more serious than usual. I waved a little and she didn't wave back. She just stared at me. I couldn't tell if she was still mad or just trying to focus on the race.

The judge called for the runners to take their marks for the 400. Mara didn't move. Finally, at the last second, she took her

position at the starting line.

Both Mara and Deb started off well. Then Deb pulled ahead. Suddenly, though, Mara caught Deb after 200 meters.

The crowd went wild. Through 300 meters, Mara and Deb were even. As they came down the homestretch, I could see their faces clearly. Deb was straining now. She was giving it everything she had. Mara was as calm and steady as ever. Then I saw Mara shift into high gear. She inched ahead.

But Deb wasn't out of it yet. She wasn't about to quit. They still had 50 meters to go. Deb was tired, though, and it started to show. She slowed down and Mara surged ahead. Finally, all of Mara's endless hours of practice paid off. She broke the tape three meters ahead of Deb Flannagan. She won!

A mob of kids surrounded Mara, cheering. I turned and saw Deb. She was bent over, gasping for air. Her eyes were filled with tears. For the first time in my life, I felt kind of sorry for her.

Then she saw me. She put her old look of confidence back on her face. But I could see she was faking it. She said, "I hope your friend knows her win was an accident. This will never happen again."

I smiled and said, "It wasn't an accident, Deb. And you know it. Mara works hard at it. You never do. You take it for granted that no one can beat you. Well, today someone did. Mara."

I stood by the door to the locker room, waiting for Mara to show up. I wanted to congratulate her. I also wanted to see if she would forgive me.

When Mara finally appeared, tons of girls came running down the hall, screaming congratulations at her. They couldn't stop talking about the great race, and they all decided to go out for pizza to celebrate. Then Deb caught up to them.

Deb said to Mara, "Hey, Two! You really lucked out today!"

Mara said, "It wasn't luck, Deb. I worked hard to win that race."

"Oh, so you think you're a big star now, huh?" said Deb.

"I won a race. That's all."

I saw Deb look at Mara with hate in her eyes. Then she turned to the other girls standing around them. "Hey, you guys. I'm going to get a burger. Who's coming with me?"

Mara said, "We're going out for pizza, Deb. Why don't you come with us?"

Deb looked at Mara for a long time. Nobody seemed to breathe.

"Deb, it's not personal," said Mara. "You'll have another shot at me at the All-City Meet. Why don't we work out together?"

"Oh, so you're the captain now?"

Mara didn't say anything.

"Come on you guys, let's get out of these smelly clothes and go get that burger." Deb pushed open the door to the locker room and let it slam behind her.

One by one, the girls on the team walked into the locker room. Then it was just Mara and me standing in the hall.

Mara looked at me.

I said, "I'm sorry."

Mara shrugged "It's OK. Deb was never my friend. You are. You're the only one who believed in me. I was afraid to go out in front of everyone and really try to win. It's easier not to try so hard. Thanks, Benny."

Chapter 4

TEAMWORK

None of the girls on the team spoke to Mara for a week after her victory. Mara didn't let it get to her, though. It just made her more determined to win. We went back to our training schedule. She worked out even harder than she had before.

Three days before the All-City Meet, Mara and I were working out as usual. We were all alone on the track.

I sensed someone standing behind me. It was Deb.

She walked over to Mara and said, "OK, 400 meters. You call the start, Benny."

"This isn't fair, Deb. You can't race Mara now! She's tired from working out and you're fresh."

"It's OK, Benny," Mara said, "Call the start."

Well, I won't rub it in. I called the start, and Mara beat Deb again. Deb was so far behind when Mara crossed the finish that she just quit

and walked away, head down. I hate to admit it, but it was pretty sad.

The day of the All-City competition came quickly. The girls' team was competing in the 4 x 400-meter relay, where four girls run as a team. Each girl runs one 400-meter leg of the race. She hands off a baton (basically a stick) to the next runner, who runs the next 400 meters. The last runner is almost always the fastest runner on the team.

When I saw Deb line up as the last runner, I almost threw up. Mara was the fastest, and Deb knew it!

But then Deb tapped Mara on the shoulder and they both went over to Coach Daltry. I wondered what was up.

The starter wondered the same thing. He called to Ms. Daltry. She signaled to wait for a moment.

Then, all of a sudden, Deb ran to the starting place. She was going first. I knew then that she had given the final 400 meters to Mara. I couldn't believe it.

The race began. Deb made great time. The next two runners on our team were a little slower. When Mara got the baton, she was behind the other teams by five or six meters.

Then, little by little, Mara started to catch up. On the last 100 meters, Mara tore out way ahead and they won!

It was an unbelievable day. The girls on the team lifted Mara and carried her around the track. Everyone cheered.

That night there was an awards ceremony. The individual winners of the different races received medals that hung on ribbons, just like in the Olympics. Mara received one for her victory in the 400. I've never seen her so happy. She got teary-eyed, and she could barely say, "Thank you."

Deb got medals in the 50- and 100-meter dashes.

Our school was the overall winner of the meet, and we got a large gold trophy. Since Deb was the captain, she accepted the award. She started off in her usual way. She bragged and flashed a smile. She raised the award high over her head. Then she got very serious. She thanked Mara for winning the 400-meter relay, which is what really won the track meet for our school.

She said, "Mara taught me a lesson about hard work and dedication. Mara trains harder than anyone else on the team." Then Deb put on a goofy grin and said, "Especially me! But that's all going to change!"

We all groaned and cried out, "Sure it will, Deb!"

"Honest!" Deb shouted with a laugh.

Then Deb asked Mara to join her on the stage. The crowd went wild.

Mara leaned in to the microphone and said, "I'd like to thank my personal trainer, whose scientific approach gave me such great results. Thanks, Benny!"

I was yelling and clapping for her. It was a very emotional moment. I hope I didn't embarrass myself!

Mara was waving and people were taking her picture. I think she was finally getting used to the attention. It was about time.

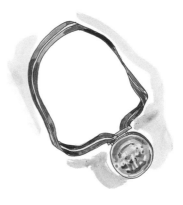